Ling and the
Little Devils

First published in Great Britain by
Pelham Books Ltd
44 Bedford Square
London WC1B 3DP
1984

First published in Denmark by Gyldendalske Boghandel
as *Ling og de små djævle* in 1984

Svend, Otto S.
Ling and the little devils.
I. Title II. Ling og de små djævle. *English*
839.8'1374[J] PZ7

ISBN 0 7207 1564 4

Printed in Denmark

SVEND OTTO S.

Ling and the Little Devils

Translated by Joan Tate

PELHAM

Ling lived in a small village in South China. His family was very poor, so poor they had very few clothes and hardly any rice. Robbers had stolen the rice they had kept to eat – and also the rice they had to pay to the landowner as rent for the land. So because they could not pay in rice, the landowner's men came and took their buffalo away.

The buffalo was very important to the family. It was also Ling's friend. As a small boy, Ling had looked after it while it grazed. The buffalo worked for them all day, pulling the heavy plough. Then they all rode home on it in the evening. Now Ling and his father had to pull the wooden plough themselves through the mud of the rice fields.

The villagers had no police to protect them from robbers. They had no schools, and the landowner was the only person who could afford a teacher. Everyone in the village was poor and only a few could read even a little.

They had no doctor. But some of the old men knew about healing plants. Ling's grandfather had taught him which plants to look for and how to make medicines from them. Ling was good at it and wanted to go to school to learn more.

Rumours were going round that an army of peasants had got together to free the people. Many of the young men in the village talked about running away to join the army. But no one knew where it was. Men just appeared out of the mountains like a swarm of bees and attacked government troops and landowners.

The old people shook their heads. "It will be just the same as before. The landowners are too strong. We'll lose again and things will be even worse than before. It's probably yet another army that will rob us and take everything we've got."

One morning, the villagers woke up to the sound of shooting.
Clouds of smoke were rising over the mountains. The villagers
hurriedly packed up their few belongings and hid their animals.

Later on, two soldiers came riding into the village and the villagers went into hiding. But the soldiers put red scrolls up on the walls saying: "We are friends. We pay for any food you bring us. We are fighting for you."

The villagers crept out of their hiding places. This had never happened before. Soldiers usually just stole everything and then disappeared.

Then an amazing army of rebel soldiers came pouring in. They had homemade straw shoes, and only a few had proper uniforms. Many were wearing straw hats they'd made themselves. They looked like a lot of toadstools marching along, smiling and waving. All of them were carrying something – heavy guns, or cooking pots and pans. Right at the end came the wounded soldiers.

Ling and his friends went and talked to the soldiers. Their parents were still afraid.

"Is there anyone here who knows how to tend wounds?" the soldiers asked. The boys all pointed at Ling. "He's called 'the little doctor'," they said.

The soldiers looked in amazement at Ling. But there was no one else. One of the soldiers had a badly wounded leg, and he couldn't possibly go on with the others.

Ling ran home and asked if they could take the soldier into their home.

"Yes," said his father. "But only if you can get him up to the hut in the top field. I'm afraid to have him here in the house. If the government troops find him, they'll shoot him. And us."

Together, the children carried the soldier up to the top field. They collected grass and made a bed for him, and Ling told them which plants and leaves they should mix and boil for medicine.

As the landowner and his family had fled, the villagers all went to his house and took out the stores of grain and rice and shared them round. Then they burnt all the papers that said how much the villagers owed. Ling's father took their buffalo back home. It was all like a party. But some of the old people shook their heads. "What'll you do when the peasant army has gone?" they said. "And the others come back?"

"But we'll come back, too," said the soldiers. "More of us will come. We won't abandon the village now we've set it free."

The next day, the peasant army had gone. Kun Chu, the wounded soldier, stayed behind. They had hidden him high up above the village, on the very top terrace where they grew the maize. Every day, the children collected up small helpings of food for him. There was very little spare cloth in the village and so bandages were hard to find. Even the smallest rag was used to patch their clothes. But the children washed and dried any little piece they could find.

Ling was happy. Now he could use everything he had learnt. What had been a game before was now a real help to the wounded soldier.

One evening, after he had changed his patient's bandage and given him some food, Ling began to ask him questions. There was so much to ask about, for neither he nor any of the others had ever been outside the village.

"Are people as poor as we are in other parts of China?" he said.

"Wherever I go," said Chu. "And wherever I've been, it's always the same. The landowners and officials take the crops. Whether it's the Emperor, or robbers, or foreigners, it's the same – we have to do the work and they get rich."

"But when the rebellion is over, will we be as rich as the landowner?"

"We probably won't be rich. But we'll be paid for our work. And we'll be able to decide things for ourselves."

"Will we get schools and new houses?" asked Ling.

"Yes, we'll have schools, but it'll take time. Just think how many people there are in China. Every one of them – adults as well as children – will learn to read and write."

"If I go with you when you leave, is there anything I can do?" said Ling.

"There are lots of boys of your age in the army. We call them 'Little Devils'," said Chu. "Boys can do lots of things. They can be scouts and help with the food. And you're good at curing illnesses with your herbs."

Ling had a lot to think about that evening.

But next day, they heard that more government troops were on the way, and the villagers were frightened. "Now we'll be punished for those few days of freedom we had," the old people said.

That evening, as Ling was on his way to Chu with a bowl of rice, two government soldiers caught him. However much he twisted and turned, he couldn't get away.

"Where are you going with that rice?" one of them said, snatching the bowl from him.

Ling was frightened, and for a moment didn't know what to say.

"Who is that rice for?" said the soldier.

"It's for *me*. I stole it," Ling lied. "From a neighbour. I daren't
eat it down there."

"You won't eat it here, either," said the soldier, grinning. The two
soldiers gobbled down the rice.

"Are there any strangers in the village?" they asked.

"No" said Ling. "Some soldiers came yesterday to fetch the
wounded."

"Which way did they go?"

"North," said Ling, pointing.

"Go on down to the village, and tell them we're coming tomorrow,"
said the soldier. As there were only two of them, they were
scared of going into the village in the dark. "Tell them we want
chickens and ducks, because we're hungry."

"The others have eaten everything," said Ling.

"We'll find what's there, all right," said the soldiers. Then they
disappeared.

Ling didn't dare go on up to Chu. Maybe the two strangers were watching him somewhere in the dark. He had an idea. He hurried home and ran from house to house to find his friends. Then they all slipped away from the village, taking with them the fireworks saved for the New Year party.

Some of the village dogs began to bark when they heard whispering and the sound of bare feet on the gravel. But the night was so full of sounds, luckily no one woke up.

When the children had gone across the rice fields and got as far as the first trees, they gathered together and Ling told them of his plan.

"When we get to the first mountain, we'll spread out and run north. Then I'll let off the first firework. We must light some bonfires, too, so the fire can be seen by the government troops.

"When the soldiers wake up, they'll think it's the rebels shooting. And they'll head that way.

"But before they even get there, we'll already be in the woods. Let off fireworks as you run north, and make sure no one sees you.

"When it's light, hide until the soldiers have gone. Don't come back until it all quietens down."

Then the children vanished into the dark between the trees.

That night, a shot was heard and sudden flashes of light appeared up in the mountains. The alarm was sounded down in the camp and the soldiers hurriedly got ready for action.

Bangs and crashes could be heard inside the woods and lights glinted here and there. The government troops thought there were hundreds of rebels on the mountains.

As the soldiers got nearer, the children fled, letting off fireworks as they went. The soldiers followed, shouting and shooting blindly. So they were led further and further away from the village.

Late the next day, the children all returned home, one by one,
tired, scratched, and blackened by gunpowder.

That was the last time government troops came to the village.
When Chu was well again, Ling and one of his friends went with
him to become one of the Little Devils.

This all happened fifty years ago, at the time when an army of peasants, workers and soldiers freed their countrymen from centuries of oppression.

For two years, they fought in the marshes, in the forests and the steep mountain crags, taking towns and villages. They walked over twelve thousand kilometres, almost a third of the distance round the whole world. This went down in history under the name of THE LONG MARCH.

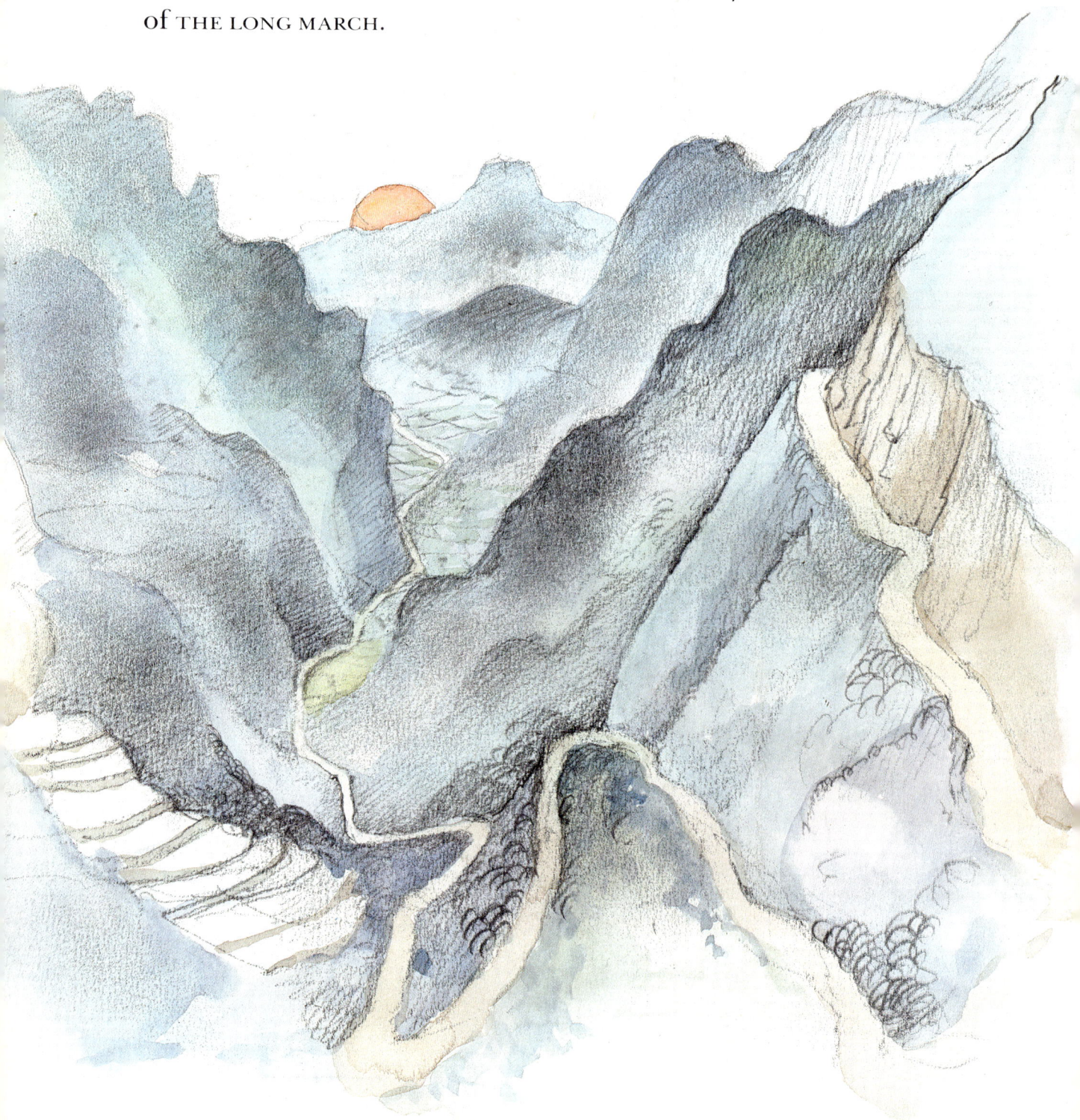